F. Day

On the Fishes of Weston-super-Mare

F. Day

On the Fishes of Weston-super-Mare

Reprint of the original, first published in 1879.

1st Edition 2024 | ISBN: 978-3-38671-477-8

Antigonos Verlag is an imprint of Outlook Verlagsgesellschaft mbH.

Verlag (Publisher): Outlook Verlag GmbH, Zeilweg 44, 60439 Frankfurt, Deutschland
Vertretungsberechtigt (Authorized to represent): E. Roepke, Zeilweg 44, 60439 Frankfurt, Deutschland
Druck (Print): Libri Plureos GmbH, Friedensallee 273, 22763 Hamburg, Deutschland

7. On the Fishes of Weston-super-Mare.
By F. DAY, F.Z.S.

[Received November 18, 1879.]

(Plates LXI. & LXII.)

Having visited Weston-super-Mare in July this year, and remained there throughout most of August, I directed my attention to the sea-fishes of that place, which, situated on the estuary of the Severn and the Wye as it enters the British Channel, is a locality too well known to call for any description : for the same reason I have deemed it unnecessary to allude to the remarkably high spring tides which occur. The amount of fishing going on was inconsiderable, boating apparently being a more profitable occupation. The shrimpers were daily at work; while stakes in narrow passes permitted the erection of stationary nets, into which small fishes and Crustacea were swept by an ebbing tide. Here I obtained most of my specimens ; but the place so swarms with crabs (*Carcinus mænas*, Linn.), that numerous little fishes were found partially devoured when the tide had ebbed sufficiently to permit the nets being examined. During the end of the first week in August, enclosures of a semicircular form were erected on the sands for the purpose of capturing flat fish (Pleuronectids). The one that appeared to be most successful was about 200 yards in length, the stakes raised to about three feet above the ground; and to these a long net was affixed.

I daily went to the stake- and shrimp-nets, as well as to the enclosures on the sands already referred to.

In drawing up this paper I took as my groundwork Mr. W. Baker's (of Bridgewater) 'Fishes of Somersetshire,'[1] including Mr. Higgins's[2] Remarks upon the Fishes of Weston-super-Mare, which he collected between the end of June and November 27, 1860. I likewise examined the specimens in the Taunton Museum, and the more extensive collection in that of Weston[3].

The fishermen complained that the season had been an unprecedently bad one, but that at times fishes had appeared most unexpectedly. This they could not account for, nor even propose any solution. Later on (September) large numbers of Soles were found to be present in the Channel, which had not been suspected ; and many that were taken weighed as much as four pounds each.

Reports from various sources lead one to the conclusion that

---

[1] Somersetshire Archæological and Natural History Society, 1851.

[2] 'Zoologist,' 1861.

[3] This Museum is under Mr. Mable, to whom belongs most of the credit for its ever having been instituted. Commencing life as a shoemaker, he first set up a school for the poorest class. He also collected the materials from which the Museum has sprung, of which he is now Curator, as well as Principal of the Institution attached to it.

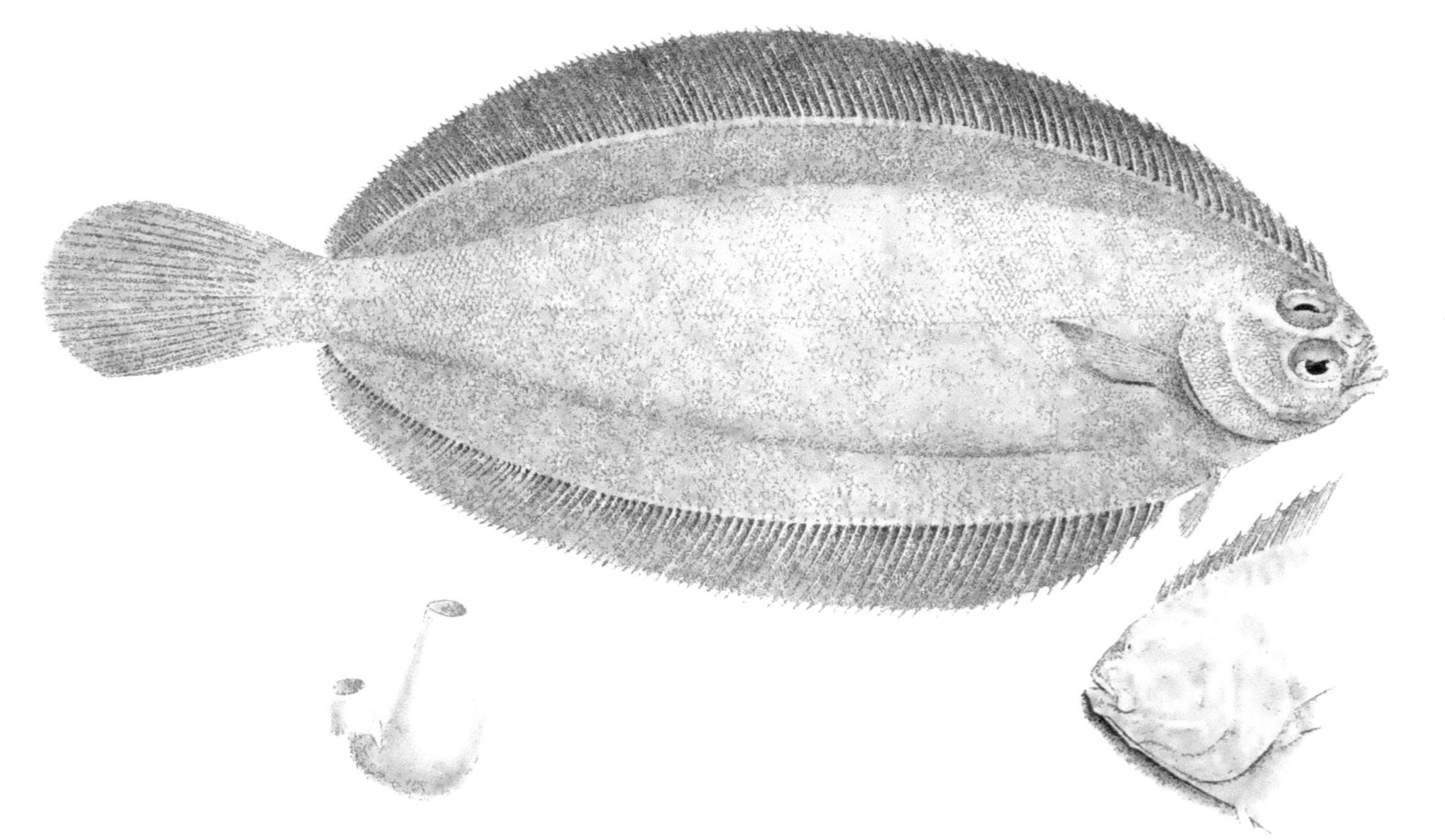

P.Z.S.1879.Pl LXI
C.Achilles del et lith
Mintern Bros imp
PLEURONECTES ELCNGATUS

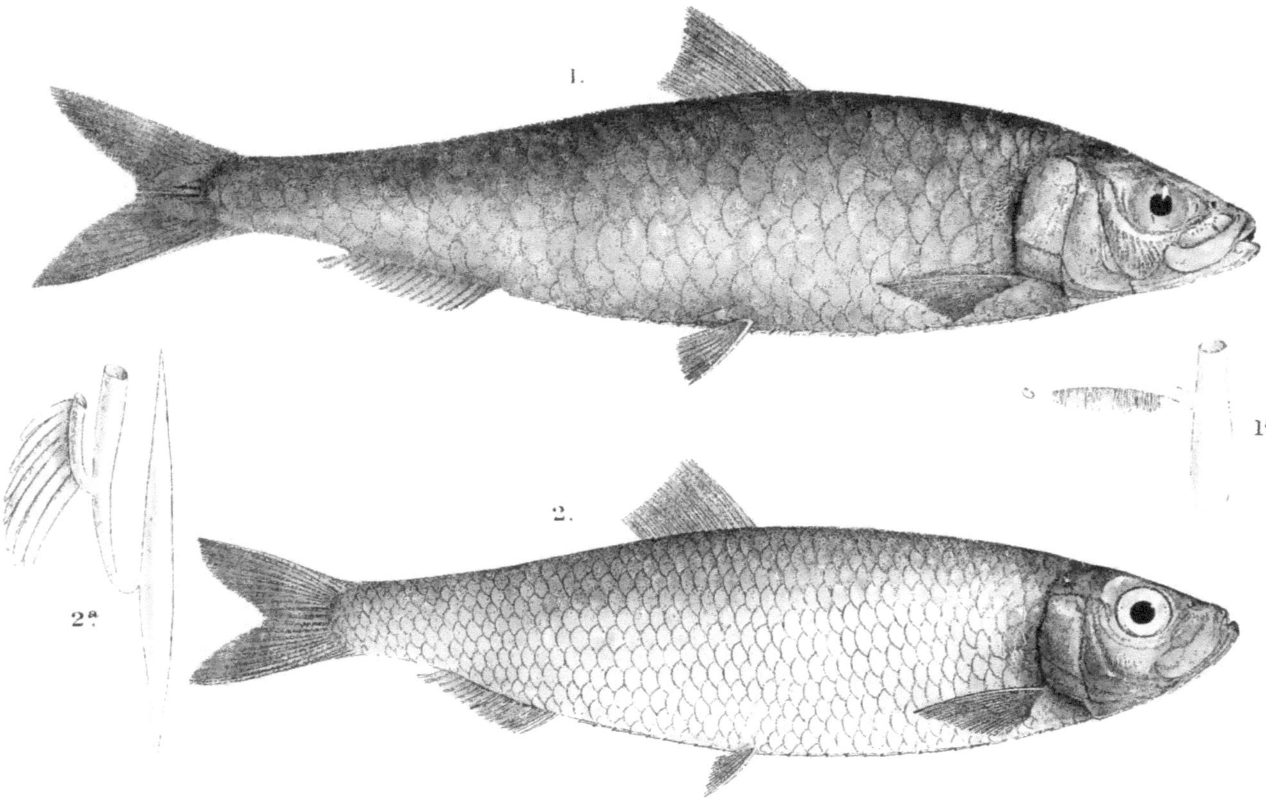

P.Z.S. 1879. Pl.LXII.
Mintern Bros. imp.
1ᵃ.
1.
2.
2ᵃ.
C.Achilles.del et lith.
1.CLUPEA PILCHARDUS. 2.CLUPEA SPRATTUS.

the migration of marine and littoral species of fish this year has been rather peculiar. Along the coast of France some forms have almost forsaken their usual haunts, but appeared in other stations, from which they had in former seasons been almost absent. Captain Salmond, of the 'Charlotte and Jane,' observes, respecting his fishing-voyages to the North Sea this year:—"It turns out, up to the time I write (June 2nd), that it is a failure in regard to Soles; also the offal is not so plentiful as in other summers. At Heligoland the fishermen have had a bad time, some being on the brink of starvation." It was stated in the papers during October that "Eastern Siberia has been suffering from famine, no whales or fish having visited those waters this summer."

Temperature is well known to exert a great influence on the migration of fishes, while we are aware of having experienced a long and severe winter, followed by a very cold spring and a comparatively colder summer. This may to a considerable extent account for the abnormal manner in which the distribution (not general supply) of marine forms has occurred throughout the last season. I therefore deem it advisable to give the temperature of the air as observed at the Royal Observatory, Greenwich, and for which I am indebted to W. Ellis, Esq.

Deviation of Mean Temperature from Average of 20 Years.

November	1878	....	$-3{\cdot}0$
December	,,	....	$-7{\cdot}1$
January	1879	....	$-6{\cdot}9$
February	,,	....	$-1{\cdot}5$
March	,,	....	$-0{\cdot}3$
April	,,	....	$-4{\cdot}3$
May	,,	....	$-4{\cdot}7$
June	,,	....	$-2{\cdot}9$
July	,,	....	$-4{\cdot}5$
August	,,	....	$-2{\cdot}0$

The above figures show that the temperature of the air has been below the average of that experienced during the last twenty years in every month referred to.

While engaged on this paper, by the kindness of the Earl of Ducie, F.R.S., I have been permitted to examine and make use of the diary kept by his lordship while on the yachting-tours which he has for several successive seasons made to Ballinskellig Bay, in Ireland, situated on the same latitude as Greenwich and Weston-super-Mare. The notes are so complete and interesting that I cannot but regret merely giving a summary, for such accurate data are probably unattainable elsewhere. During the last four years fishing has been done from a 30-ton cutter, but in 1873 and 1874 from yacht-boats. The takes have been as follows :—

Species.	1873.	1874.	1876.	1877.	1878.	1879.
Red Mullet	27	11	1	4	1	2
Sea-Bream	61	13	176	210	57	1
Red Gurnard	...	...	20	18	12	7
Sapphirine Gurnard	...	...	24	29	59	71
Grey Gurnard	...	...	95	54	78	178
Piper	...	...	4	1	...	9
Mackerel	222	118	110	2	108	...
Dory	1	4	5	4	5	27
Cod, over 5 lb.	...	...	14	4	4	3
Whiting	84	124	170	306	114	310
Whiting Pout	95	10	32	6	12	8
Pollack, over 4 lb.	...	...	33	19	43	11
Hake	...	...	...	...	...	2
Ling	9	13	22	23	15	14
Turbot	1	4	15	115	47	57
Brill	4	...	16	29	34	92
Whiff	...	...	7	7	2	4
Plaice	51	147	199	582	374	1032
Dab	...	...	56	77	54	326
Lemon Dab	...	...	13	8	5	20
Flounder	...	...	19	43	51	38
Sole	51	147	250	289	403	683
Lemon Sole	...	...	7	9	7	2
Conger	86	56	22	29	43	6

If we divide the fishes captured in the years 1878 and 1879 into families, we find as follows :—

	1878.	1879.
Mullidæ	1	2
Sparidæ	57	1
Triglidæ	149	265
Carangidæ	113	28
Gadidæ	188	348
Pleuronectidæ	977	1954
Muraenidæ	43	6

One cause which has great bearing upon the presence or absence of certain kinds of fish is, as already observed, the temperature of the sea. The following figures from Lord Ducie's notes show what was the average temperature at the surface daily at 7 A.M. :—

| 1878, July | 63° | August .. | 61·8° |
| 1879, „ | 53·5 | „ .. | 56·8 |

Consequently in July 1879 we find the temperature of the air was 4°·5 lower than the average of the mean temperature for the last twenty years, and of the surface-water of the sea 9°·5 less than in 1878 ; while in August the mean temperature of the air was 2°·0 less than the average for the last twenty years, and of the surface-water of the sea 5° lower than in 1878.

On July 21, 1878, at 12.30 A.M., the temperature of the sea is thus recorded :—At surface, 71° ; at 1 fathom, 67°·5 ; 2 fathoms, 66° ;

3 fathoms, 65°; 4 fathoms, 63°; 5 fathoms, 61°; 6 fathoms, 60°; 7 fathoms (at bottom), 59°.

If I now confine my figures to the temperature and species of fishes taken by trawling solely in Ballinskellig Bay in 1878 and 1879, I find as follows:—Trawling was only employed on four days in July 1878, in from 3 to 5 fathoms of water, with the surface-temperature at 7 A.M. 60° to 62°, or having an average of 61°: the total captures were:—7 Sapphirine Gurnards; 1 Dory; 18 Turbot; 11 Brill; 99 Plaice; 11 Dabs; 11 Flounders; 157 Soles; 2 Lemon Soles. In August 1878 trawling was employed on 15 days, with the surface-temperature at 7 A.M. 60° to 64°, giving an average of 62°. It was remarked on August 7th that four scrapes were taken with a 16-foot beam-trawl, and that the Plaice captured nearly doubled the Soles in number, probably due to the speed at which the boat was driven, and to the elevation of the "head-rope" above the ground, as effected by the trawl-beam. Two of the scrapes were in 3 fathoms and two in 5 fathoms of water; but there was no very marked difference in the result. The total captures in the 15 days of August were as follows:—1 Bass; 2 Sea-Bream; 31 Sapphirine Gurnards; 3 Grey Gurnards; 4 Dory; 18 Mackerel; 34 Turbot; 28 Brill; 194 Plaice; 25 Dabs; 23 Flounders; 246 Soles; 1 Lemon Sole.

In the year 1879, trawling was employed for 12 days in July, with the surface-temperature at 7 A.M. 50° to 56°, having an average of 53°·9. The total captures were:—1 Sea-Bream; 2 Sapphirine Gurnards; 2 Grey Gurnards; 8 Dory; 2 Angler; 2 Ling; 25 Turbot; 32 Brill; 393 Plaice; 117 Dabs; 4 Lemon Dabs; 2 Flounders; 229 Soles; 1 Lemon Sole; 4 Whiffs. During August trawling was carried on 11 days, with the surface-temperature at 7 A.M. 54° to 58°, having a mean of 56°·5. The total captures were:—9 Sapphirine Gurnards; 5 Grey Gurnards; 4 Piper; 12 Dory; 1 Angler; 19 Turbot; 45 Brill; 448 Plaice; 137 Dabs; 5 Lemon Dabs; 4 Flounders; 269 Soles. We find, therefore, that the fishes captured in the two years were about as follows :—

	Bass.	Sea-Bream.	Gurnards.	Dory.	Mackerel.	Angler.	Gadidæ.	Pleuronec-toids.
July 1878, 4 days, mean temp. 7 A.M. 61° ..	...	...	7	1	...	...	...	309
„ 1879, 12 days, „ „ „ 53·9...	...	1	4	1	...	1	1	807
Aug. 1878, 15 days, „ „ „ 62 ...	1	2	34	4	18	...	...	551
„ 1879, 9 days[1], „ „ „ 56·5...	...	1	4	8	...	2	2	807

[1] Trawling was resorted to on eleven days, but only on nine of them have I the numbers of each species captured.

There appear to have been less Gurnards taken in the 21 days' trawling in 1879 than in the 19 days in 1878 ; more Dory (9 instead of 5); no Mackerel (in place of 18 in 1878); but a very much larger number of Pleuronectoids, 1614 in place of 860 in 1878. Still one must not attribute the increase of Soles caught entirely to a local augmentation in the number of fish in the sea, as, in the first place, the " sweep " of the trawl was as 5 to 4, being 50 feet " spread " in 1879 instead of 40 feet in 1878. The bridles, *i. e.* the ropes to the " Otter heads," or weighted wooden kites, which run along the bottom, were rather better adjusted in 1879 ; while the weather for working the trawl was more propitious, consequently it was more frequently employed. A depth of about 5 fathoms was found to be most favourable in 1879, whereas in warmer seasons 3 to $3\frac{1}{2}$ fathoms have been found to yield the best captures. The facilities for the different kinds of fishing varied with the weather : thus the takes of Whiting show fine weather, when line-fishing could be attempted outside the Bay.

Although many deductions might be drawn from Lord Ducie's notes, I propose deferring them for the present, in the hope of obtaining the general returns of the sea-fisheries of the United Kingdom. It would, however, appear that among the Soles and flat fishes generally, striking anomalies in distribution have occurred during the past season. They would seem to have more or less forsaken (for a time, at least) the North Sea, and to have appeared in augmented numbers on the S.W. coast of Ireland and the Bristol Channel. Whether the temperature of the sea in certain localities has been so low as to cause the migration of the food of these fishes, or the fishes themselves have been acted on by cold, through the medium of the water, or both causes have combined, are questions worth investigating, but which I propose to defer for the present.

Passing on to the fishes themselves, I have added remarks to many species, frequently made, as will be observed, in other localities than at Weston.

Labrax lupus, Lacép.   The Bass.

I obtained several small examples, none of which exceeded a pound in weight. All were from the stationary shrimp-nets. It is observed, in Lord Ducie's diary, on August 10, 1878, that " in the North Bay the Bass were hunting the Sprats to the surface, the Gulls assisting. This went on all day, along the strand up to the embouchure of the Jung River."

Polyprion cernium, Val.   Stone-Bass.
Somersetshire (*Baker*).

Mullus surmuletus, Linn.
M. barbatus, De La Roche.
Somersetshire (*Baker*).
Lord Ducie took two examples on August 2nd this year in a trammel set in Ballinskellig Bay ; while one was likewise similarly captured July 26, 1878.

PAGRUS VULGARIS, Cuv. & Val.
Somersetshire (*Baker*).

PAGELLUS CENTRODONTUS, De La Roche.   Sea-Bream.
Somersetshire (*Baker*).

COTTUS SCORPIUS, Bloch.   Sting-fish or Sea-Scorpion.
This fish is taken at Weston during the winter.   I have received
several examples, captured at Southend, at the mouth of the Thames,
from Mr. Carrington, naturalist to the Royal Westminster Aquarium.
The spines at the preopercular angle are occasionally reduced from
three to two, while the usual number of the dorsal spines is 10, and
of the anal rays 10 instead of 11 or 12.

COTTUS BUBALIS, Euphr.   Father Lasher or Long-spined Sea-
Scorpion.
C. grœnlandicus, Cuv. & Val.; *C. labradoricus*, Girard; *C. ocel-
latus*, Storer.
The American form or variety is said to have " the ridges of the
bones of the head tubercular, not covered with skin " (Günther,
Catal. ii. p. 165).   I find the same appearances in some examples
received from Southend.   The variety of *Cottus scorpius* mentioned
by Couch as having a " row of tendrils hanging from the skin above
the eyes " was probably an example of this species, which usually
has a few short tentacles about the head and above the eyes, while
there is frequently rather a large one at the outer end of the maxilla.

TRIGLA CUCULUS, Linn.   Elleck or Red Gurnard.
T. pini, Bloch.
Occasionally taken at Weston.

TRIGLA LINEATA, Gmel.; Linn.   Streaked Gurnard.
This, as well as the next two, are occasionally captured.   This fish
is said to be very seldom taken by a bait.   Mr. Cornish ('Zoologist,'
1878, p. 423) observes that it is never taken on a hook.   At the
Westminster Aquarium I observe that these fishes become quite as
tame as the other forms, taking pieces of mussel or shrimps as well
as any other fish, and apparently with as little fear.

TRIGLA HIRUNDO, Bloch.   Sapphirine Gurnard.
T. pœciloptera, Cuv. & Val.

TRIGLA GURNARDUS, Linn.   Grey Gurnard.
T. cuculus, Bloch; *T. blochii*, Yarrell.
I received one example from Mr. Carrington, captured at Southend, in which the white spots have run into narrow and sinuous
lines, while a black blotch, surrounded by a light ring, exists on the
first dorsal fin.   The colours in this species vary exceedingly : in
some there are no white spots, the upper half of the body being of
a slate-grey, conjoined with which a black blotch usually exists on

the first dorsal fin (*T. blochii*). This dorsal blotch, however, as a rule, is present in all specimens, although in some it is faint, or merges into the colour of the remainder of the fin, while it frequently becomes lost in examples kept long in spirit. Occasionally the dorsal blotch instead of being round is semicircular.

This is said to be the most common form of Gurnard at Weston; but none of the genus were captured when I was there. Although Couch observes that *T. gurnardus* is less sensible to variations in temperature than any other form of British Gurnard, it is found to be the most difficult to keep alive in the Westminster Aquarium.

TRIGLA LYRA, Linn.   The Piper.

Somersetshire (*Baker*).
Scouler (Mag. Nat. Hist. vi. 1833, p. 529) states this fish not to be rare at Glasgow, where it sometimes attains to 7 lb. weight. Lord Ducie found it this year more abundant than usual in Ballinskellig Bay, where in August he obtained nine with the trawl, in 1878 none, in 1877 one, in 1876 four.

AGONUS CATAPHRACTUS, Linn.   The Pogge.
A local example exists in the Weston Museum.

TRACHINUS DRACO, Linn.   Great Weever.
A single local example in the Weston Museum.

TRACHINUS VIPERA, Cuv. & Val.   Little Weever.
I obtained a single specimen from the stationary fish-nets. The fishermen professed to regard these fish as very rare.

SCOMBER SCOMBER, Linn.   The Mackerel.

A few (adult) are occasionally taken near Weston. Mr. Dunn, of Megavissey, observes (MS.) that "many have the fins of the belly red. Our fishermen carefully note them, as when they appear quantities of fish are always off the coast. * * * Their ova float on the surface of the sea. * * * During the month of September this year some hundreds of a fish-louse (*Rocinela dannoniensis*[1]) have been found on the Mackerel at Megavissey; all I have noticed or heard of have, except in one instance, been taken from near the pectoral fins; the one excepted was imbedded in a wound near the vent of the fish. These 'Lice,' as our fishermen call them, visit our coasts in countless millions in the spring months of the year; they seldom come nearer than 3 miles from the shore, and remain on the sea-bottom. Sea-Bream eat them readily."

In the ‘Field’ (August 9th) is an account of another Isopod, *Æga tridens*, and its carnivorous propensities. It is there stated, by both Mr. Tudor and Mr. Anderson, that in Shetland they attack the fish caught on the long lines, when laid on certain sandy bottoms or grounds, and, getting in through the gills, it is supposed, eat up the inside of the fish without destroying the skin or bone, so that

[1] Mr. Miers has kindly identified the species.

when the fish is hauled up it looks as plump and round as a live fish, but when opened is found full of these parasites.

Mr. Dunn subsequently (Sept. 29th) observes, "the statement in the 'Field' is quite in keeping with our knowledge of these fish-lice. We have no deep-sea long lines in use here; our deep-sea fishing is done with hand-lines; consequently we have no opportunity of testing the habits of the 'lice' in a like manner with the northern fishermen. But it often happens when a half Mackerel is used as a bait that the lice will in a few minutes scoop out all the fish, leaving nothing but the skeleton and the skin. To a novice, the bait will appear as round and full as when first cast into the sea, so closely packed are the lice in the body, but a hard rap against the side of the boat reveals the secret. They give out a ticking sound when crawling."

ZEUS FABER, Linn.   John Dory or Doree.

I obtained two from the stationary shrimp-nets. This fish has numerous yellow lines taking an irregular horizontal direction along the body, a very light edging to the black lateral blotch, and two darkish lines along both dorsal and anal fins. At the Westminster Aquarium these fish are fed upon Sand-Smelts; and one day, being perhaps more hungry than usual, a Dory was observed to seize a young Bass, which it subsequently devoured. Mr. Saville Kent drew attention to the peculiar manner in which this fish uses its fins, which he, with great justice, likens to that of the dorsal fin in the Pipe-fish, a movement that Dr. J. E. Gray considered resembled the action of the Archimedean screw. This rapid motion affects the soft rays and interradial membrane of the dorsal, anal, and pectoral fins, all, or merely some, of which may be in motion at the same time. This may be perceived both when they are ascending or descending, or even when lying over on one side; but they are likewise able to move their fins more slowly, as we generally perceive in fishes.

The Dory appears to have been more common this year than usual. Turning to Lord Ducie's captures, I find them in Ballinskellig Bay as follows :—1873, one; 1874, four; 1876, five; 1877, four; 1878, five; 1879, twenty-seven.

CAPROS APER, Linn.   The Boar-fish.

An example, $5\frac{1}{4}$ inches in length, is in the Weston Museum; it was brought there alive. Large numbers have been captured this year off the English coast; and Mr. Carrington observes that he has received notices, during June 1879, of their having been taken in various parts of the south and south-east coast of England. At Weymouth and Bournemouth they were not infrequently found dead on the shore. At Sheerness a shrimp-trawler took a dozen at one draught; off Harwich a pair were similarly captured. The Essex fishermen term them 'Red Dorees,' but do not remember observing them in previous years. In the commencement of September, about a dozen were captured in one day on the south coast. Mr. Dunn sent me a fine example from Megavissey, November this year. On examining it, I found three cæcal appendages, whereas this fish is usually stated only to possess two.

XIPHIAS GLADIUS, Linn.   The Sword-fish.

The cast of an example exists in the Weston Museum, taken by Mr. Mable from a specimen 9 feet long, which was captured near the town, at Burnham, in the summer of 1873.   Its snout and fins are likewise preserved.   On its left side, opposite the hind edge of the first anal fin, existed a large cicatrix, evidently due to a wound, which had nearly transfixed the fish, there being a spot on the opposite side showing to where the injury had extended.   It does not seem improbable that this wound may have been inflicted by another individual of the same species.   In the daily newspapers the capture of one of these fish in the Wye, on October 9th, is announced.   It strayed up during the night, and was left stranded at Chepstow on the ebb making.   Length 8 feet 6 inches; snout 3 feet long; weight 200 lb.

I was particularly desirous of examining the Gobies of Weston, as Couch has figured and described several supposed new species or Mediterranean forms from that locality.   Every ichthyologist will admit the difficulty of solving questions of species, especially among Gobies, when the author omits to mention the number of the fin-rays, makes no remarks on the scales or teeth, while the size of the published figures does not accord with that of the specimen as described in the text.   Finding myself completely at a loss, I determined to collect these fishes at Weston, whence *the Yellow Goby, the One-spotted Goby, the Speckled Goby, the Transparent Goby*, and the *Slender Goby* had been obtained.   While demurring to the value of some of these species, it must not be overlooked that in the following identifications of Couch's text and plates I have had to be guided very considerably by colour and form, while, on the other hand, our examples came from the same locality.

GOBIUS MINUTUS, Gmel., Linn.; Donovan, pl. xxxviii.; Yarrell; Parnell.

This species was very numerous; some examples agreed with *G. unipunctatus*, Parnell, and *One-spotted Goby*, Couch, and probably *G. gracilis*, Jenyns; while the *Tail-spotted Goby* of Couch is perhaps the young.

GOBIUS RUTHENSPARRI, Euph.

Not uncommon.   Couch's *Two-spotted Goby* is this species, while his *Broad-finned Goby* may be the male.

GOBIUS RHODOPTERUS, Günther.

Not rare.   It is identical with *G. minutus*, Couch, and *G. gracilis*, Parnell and Yarrell (not Jenyns).   The female differs considerably in colour from the male, while its fins are lower.   It appears to be the *Yellow Goby* of Couch, not of Risso.

Couch gives a *Transparent Goby* and a *Slender Goby*, which may be examples of *Latrunculus albus*, a fish he considered "as the young of some better known species."

CALLIONYMUS LYRA, Linn.   *C. dracunculus*, Linn. (female). The Dragonet, Gemmous and Sordid Dragonets.

This fish is taken off Weston, but only the male exists in the Museum.   Mr. Sandford, to whom I am indebted for assistance in my investigations at the excellent Taunton Museum, informs me that the Skulpin is very good eating.

CYCLOPTERUS LUMPUS, Linn.   Lump-sucker.

This fish is said to arrive in the cold months, and commits considerable havoc among the sprats.

"Watching a Lump-sucker firmly attached to the glass of the tank, the idea occurred to me that the sucker may have been developed by natural selection, as a useful adjunct to the breathing movements of the fish.   When fixed, the fish appears to be perfectly at ease, and to breathe more fully and strongly than when swimming.   The movements of the opercles or gill-covers, when the fish was attached, were specially strong, as compared with their motion in the act of swimming.   In a large-headed and heavy-bodied fish, like *Cyclopterus*, any aid given to the respiratory movements would be a clear gain to the animal ; and from a habit of simply resting on a object, so as to afford leverage and play to the gills, the comparatively useless ventral fins may have become specially modified as a disk of attachment ; the development of the sucking-disk, and enlargement of the branchial cavity, would thus proceed *pari passu*, and by natural selection the present exaggerated features of both organs would be attained."   (A. Wilson, 'Nature,' June 26, 1879, p. 197.)   I would suggest that this modification of the ventral fins into a sucker (as we observe the first dorsal similarly modified in *Echeneis*) is principally for adhesion, either to prevent their being carried away by the tide, or to attach themselves to their prey.   A heavy body, as a Lump-sucker, violently rolled over by a strong wave, would be liable to suffer considerable injury.   As a proof of this I would refer to Dr. McIntosh, who observes that after storms these fishes are found on the west sands of St. Andrews.

LIPARIS VULGARIS, Flem.   Sea-Snail.

Small examples I found exceedingly common at Weston, several being almost invariably present in every shrimp-net, while the crabs appeared to be uncommonly fond of them, few being uninjured.   In none could I see any blue lines.   Large examples are said to be common in the winter.

LIPARIS MONTAGUI, Donovan.

Has been recorded from Somersetshire.

LOPHIUS PISCATORIUS, Linn.   Angler ; Fishing-Frog.

Every two or three years a large one is taken at Weston.   The cast of one 4 feet long is in the Museum, as well as the jaws of two or three adults.

CEPOLA RUBESCENS, Linn. The Band-fish.

Somersetshire (*Baker*).

A specimen from Exmouth, captured this year and given me by Frank Buckland, Esq., was infested with worms, which Mr. Cobbold found to be examples of Rudolphi's so-called *Nematoideum cepolæ-rubescentis.* Six different internal parasites have been described from this fish.

BLENNIUS GATTORUGINE, Bloch.

Local examples of this Blenny are in the Museum.

ATHERINA PRESBYTER, Cuv. Sand-Smelt.

MUGIL CAPITO, Cuv. The Grey Mullet.

I saw an example nearly three feet long, taken out of the flounder-stakes, they are said not to be commonly seen, but occasionally small schools of them are captured in the stationary shrimp-nets. At the Westminster Aquarium, those in the same tank as the Sturgeon greedily devoured lob-worms; their food is chopped mussels.

MUGIL SEPTENTRIONALIS, Günther. *M. chelo*, Yarrell.

Has been recorded from Somersetshire.

GASTEROSTEUS ACULEATUS, Will. The Tinker.

I obtained an example from the stationary shrimp-nets, others likewise exist in the Museum. Baker records the following varieties as found in the county :—*G. trachurus*, C. & V.; *G. semiar-matus*, C. & V.; *G. leiurus*, C. & V., or *G. gymnurus*, Cuv. Although these Sticklebacks (or Pricklebacks, as they were formerly called) are taken in both fresh and sea water, Mr. Mable found that in an aquarium they rarely lived in salt water upwards of six weeks, and even then they did not thrive. Having obtained upwards of a score, he placed them in a freshwater aquarium, which was apparently too small for all to live in together with comfort; consequently some of the weaker were eaten by the stronger and larger ones. This could not have been due to want of food, as they had as much as they wished for ; what they especially seemed to relish was butter, to obtain which they would even spring out of the water. They became exceedingly tame, and were fed with dried beef shredded, which they would take from the hand, but preferred Mrs. Mable to any one else ; in fact she had only to hold a finger over the aquarium, and they would at once come and follow it as she moved it along. Some of the most brilliant males took and retained particular stations, and from which they drove away interlopers. They constructed nests of small bits of twigs, which they carried in their mouth like birds to the place where they desired to form their domicile, which was invariably laid on a sandy foundation. As soon as a piece of stick or other substance had been deposited, the fish carried some sand in its mouth and strewed it above; then taking in some more sand, it went a short distance off and blew it over the structure, thus causing it to be diffused in a shower of bubbles. The nest when completed had its entrance on one side and its exit on the other, as has been described by Dr. Ransom and other observers; this nest, if lifted out of the aquarium, appeared to be glued together by a jelly-like substance. Mr. Warrington (Ann. & Mag. Nat. Hist. 1855, (2) xvi. p. 330) remarks that the adult die when they have pro-pagated their species.

Some Roach, *Leuciscus rutilus*, were added to the inmates of the aquarium, with which invasion the Sticklebacks did not appear to be pleased; still they were not frightened, but forthwith attacked the in-truders, biting at them anywhere and everywhere, until they became thoroughly cowed. Then these little tyrants were observed to place themselves in front of the Roach, steady themselves by their tail, and then suddenly dart straight at the lips of their intended prey, from which they bit pieces out. These attacks were continued until the Roach had been killed, when they were eaten by their conquerors.

GATEROSTEUS SPINACHIA, Linn.   Fifteen-spined Stickleback.

A local specimen exists in the Weston Museum.

LABRUS MACULATUS, Bloch.   The Ballan Wrasse.

Two local examples exist in the Weston Museum; they were received alive.

LABRUS MIXTUS, Fries, the Cook; LABRUS COMBER, Pennant; CRENILABRUS MELOPS, Linn., the Corkwing; GYMNELIS IM-BERBIS, Linn., the Beardless Ophidium. Have all been taken in Somersetshire.

AMMODYTES LANCEOLATUS, Le Sauvage.   The Greater Sand-Eel or Sand-Launce.

Baker reports this species from Somersetshire. In examining a very fine example received from Mr. Dunn, I find the œsophagus enters abruptly into a pyriform stomach, which has a very narrow prolongation from its posterior or larger end, longer than the remainder of the organ; the pylorus is also very narrow, and where it enters the small intestines that canal is prolonged upwards into a cæcal sac, while the length of the remainder of the tube scarcely exceeds half the length of the stomach.

AMMODYTES TOBIANUS, Linn.   Lesser Sand-Eel.

Found at Weston.

MORRHUA VULGARIS, Flem.   Codfish.

Taken during the winter months on lines; as is also MORRHUA ÆGLEFINUS, or the Haddock; M. MERLANGUS, Linn., or the Whiting, numbers of the young of which are captured in the shrimp-nets; and MORRHUA LUSCA, Linn., or the Bib.

GADUS POLLACHIUS, Linn., the Pollack, and MERLUCCIUS VULGARIS, or the Hake, are also occasionally taken in the Trammel during the winter months.

PHYCIS BLENNOIDES, Brünn., or the Forked Hake; MOLVA VULGARIS, Flem., or the Ling; MOTELLA MUSTELA, Linn., Five-bearded Rockling; M. TRICIRRATA, Bl., Three-bearded Rockling; RANICEPS TRIFURCATUS, Flem., Trifurcated Hake. Have all been captured in Somersetshire.

RHOMBUS MAXIMUS, Linn. The Turbot.

A few are captured off Weston; one weighed 16 lb. The following memoranda from Lord Ducie's observations on this fish, as taken in Ballinskellig Bay, are very suggestive as to the growth of the Turbot:—

In the year 1877 the average weight (excluding the three largest fish, as was done also in 1878 and 1879) was 2 lb., a few were an ounce or two above or below that weight. In the two succeeding years, captured at the same place and time, they were as follows:—

1878.			1879.		
	Weight.			Weight.	
No. of fish.	lb.	oz.	No. of fish.	lb.	oz.
...	...	...	1	1	...
4	1	8	...	...	...
...	...	...	3	1	4
...	...	...	2	1	8
2	1	12	1	1	12
2	2	...	7	2	...
...	...	...	1	2	8
1	2	10	...	...	...
1	2	12	...	...	...
18	3	...	9	3	...
2	3	4	2	3	4
9	3	8	1	3	8
...	...	...	3	3	12
1	3	14	...	...	...
1	4	...	3	4	...
1	4	4	3	4	4
...	...	...	2	4	8
...	...	...	1	4	12
...	...	...	3	5	...
...	...	...	3	5	4
...	...	...	1	5	8
...	...	...	2	5	12
...	...	...	2	6	...
...	...	...	1	6	4
...	...	...	1	6	12
1	7	...	2	7	...

If we analyze the foregoing figures we find the captures in the three years as follows:—

Weight:—	1–2 lb.	2–3 lb.	3–4 lb.	4–5 lb.	5–6 lb.	6–7 lb.	
1877 ..	111	4	..	..	..	..	or 115 fish.
1878 ..	8	20	12	2	..	1	or 43 „
1879 ..	6	8	18	9	8	4	or 53 „

The general average of the weight of the captures increased from 2 lb. in 1877, to 3 lb. in 1878, and 3 lb. 11 oz. in 1879; and an examination of the figures leads to the belief that the broods were much more numerous in the first than in the second or third year; while the small size of those taken in 1877 would also seem to infer the absence of large Turbot in Ballinskellig Bay at that time. In 1878 the figures apparently show that the increase in weight of the fish had been from $\frac{1}{2}$ to $2\frac{1}{2}$ lb. each fish, the highest numbers being among examples from 2 to 4 lb., instead of from 1 to 2 lb. But in 1879 we again find a change, the highest numbers captured being among those weighing from 3 to 5 lb. each, which would seem to confirm the conclusions demonstrable from the figures in the preceding years.

RHOMBUS LÆVIS, Linn.   The Brill.

Is occasionally taken at Weston.

RHOMBUS MEGASTOMA, Donov.   The Whiff, or Mary Sole.
RHOMBUS PUNCTATUS, Bloch.   " Muller's Topknot."
These fishes are both found in Devonshire ; the latter frequently in the spring months. In Ballinskellig Bay this year Lord Ducie took Whiffs between the middle and end of July, but none in the succeeding month.

ARNOGLOSSUS LATERNA, Walb.   The Scald-fish.

Somersetshire (*Baker*).

PLEURONECTES PLATESSA, Linn.   The Plaice.   P. LIMANDA, Linn. The Dab. PLEURONECTES MICROCEPHALUS, Donovan. The Smear Dab.

PLEURONECTES ELONGATUS, Yarrell.   (Plate LXI.)

The talented author of the 'British Fishes' received an example from Stolford in Somersetshire, where Mr. Baker obtained two specimens; and Mr. Higgins (Zoologist, 1861, p. 7317) records two more from Weston, which he gave to Mr. Couch. It is with much pleasure that I have to record my thanks to that excellent observer Mr. Matthias Dunn, of Megavissey, in Cornwall, for a fine example, about 9 inches long, taken in 30 fathoms water by a trawler, almost two miles from the Deadman, Cornwall, November 6th, 1879, and which I received on the 10th.

B. v., D. 115, P. 12, V. 6, A. 97, C. 19, L. l. 115.

Length of head $6\frac{1}{2}$, of caudal fin $6\frac{1}{2}$, height of body $3\frac{1}{4}$ in the total length. *Eyes* on the right side, and separated from each other by a very narrow scaleless ridge, which is continued almost to the origin of the lateral line; lower eye one third in advance of the upper. Lower jaw slightly the longer anteriorly, and has a tubercle below the symphysis. Maxilla two thirds as long as the orbit, and extending to beneath the front edge of the lower eye. Body very thin, its greatest thickness equalling one sixth of its greatest height, excluding the vertical fins. *Teeth* in a single row, compressed, with their crowns somewhat obtuse; teeth most developed on the blind side. *Fins.* Dorsal commences over the middle of the upper eye, its longest rays being in its middle, where they are three fifths of the length of the head; posteriorly the fin terminates almost close to the root of the caudal fin, which latter is wedge-shaped. Anal similar to dorsal, but its middle rays not so elongated. Both pectorals with twelve rays, the left half as long as the head, the right one fourth longer than the left. Ventrals each with six rays, and one half as long as the pectoral. *Scales* cycloid on left, feebly ctenoid on the right side, *none over the fin-rays* except on the caudal. *Lateral line* with very slightly oblique descent above the pectoral fin, whence it proceeds direct to centre of the caudal. *Gill-rakers* short, spinate, and widely separated. *Cæcal appendages* two, moderately developed. *Colours*: right side brown, with a slaty tinge, darkest about the head; a black blotch on the upper half of the pectoral fin; vertical fins of a greyish slate-colour, the anterior dorsal rays being tipped with white; left side white.

Habitat. A single example 9 inches long, from Megavissey, Cornwall, obtained and recognized by Mr. Matthias Dunn. Yarrell's example, a dried skin, had probably shrunk, causing it to appear more elongated than is natural. It is more closely allied to *P. cynoglossus.*

PLEURONECTES FLESUS, Linn.   The Flounder.

Reversed examples were exceedingly numerous, and in one instance I saw a Flounder coloured on both sides. I would here draw especial attention to four abnormally coloured Plaice and Flounders in the Westminster Aquarium, all of which are white on the underside; the eyes are normal; while the albinism I am about to describe has existed from the time they were received, neither increasing nor diminishing. In one (1) the dorsal and anal fins are white to a great extent, but in rather an irregular manner; (2) the dorsal and anal fins are similar to no. 1, but the white has extended onto the sides of the body; (3) the white is rather more spread than in no. 2; (4) the caudal fin and most of the posterior half of the body are nearly white, whereas the anterior portion of the body is mottled. If, as suggested by A. Agassiz, the colours of these fish are affected owing to the eye, on what will eventually be the uncoloured side, passing over to the upper surface, leaving the eyeless side colourless, due to the controlling power of the nerve having become unable to act over the colour-cells, how, one would suggest, can this albinism be present in examples wherein both eyes are present on the dark side thus affected?

SOLEA VULGARIS, Quensel.   The Sole.

Small ones were common in the shrimp-nets at Weston; and Mr. Mable writes me word from Weston (Sept. 13) that, "during the last few days, a large quantity of very fine Soles have been taken here. On inquiry I find they were caught about 30 miles down the Channel by two trawls from Cardiff; the gross weight was 10 tons, and the heaviest pair 8 lbs. This is a new fishing-ground, having only been tried about 6 months. Numbers of other fish have been taken, and recently a Sturgeon. The waters close here cannot be trawled, because cod-lines have been in use for about the last hundred years, and every time one is sunk a large stone or two is let down with it ; consequently the sea-bottom is studded with this kind of thing."

SOLEA VARIEGATA, Donov., Variegated Sole ; SOLEA VULGARIS, Günther, the Lemon Sole ; SOLEA MINUTA, Parnell, the Little Sole. Have all been recorded from Somersetshire.

MAUROLICUS BOREALIS, Nilss. The Argentine.
Seven examples taken at Weston by Higgins.

SALMO SALAR, Linn. The Salmon.
Occasionally an example gets into one of the stationary shrimp-nets in passing from the sea to the rivers or *vice versâ*. It may be observed in this place that the authorities of the Brighton Aquarium have now conclusively demonstrated, what has long been known to every ichthyologist, that the Parr is the young Salmon. Mr. Francis Francis observes in the ' Field ' (August 2, 1879) that Mr. Berrington sent from the Usk "a beautiful consignment of small Parr, to the number of about twenty, about six or eight months ago, more than three fourths of which are still alive. They were placed in fresh water, and soon began to feed and take to their tank. From that time not one has died ; towards May, most of them began to assume the Smolt stage. I think there were only four which failed to do so, all the rest became veritable Smolts ; the four remained definite Parr. Then arose the question what were we do ; should we take out the Parr and leave the Smolts ; and then introduce salt water gradually ? * * We therefore thought we would sacrifice the four Parr, if it were necessary, as the belief formerly prevailed that to introduce Parr into salt water before they assumed the Smolt stage was certain death to them."   He continued that salt water was gradually introduced ; the Smolts became rampant with pleasure while the Parr did not die. At last no fresh water remained in the tank ; it was entirely marine. "Then the Parrs which had remained Parrs up to that time began to assume the Smolt stage, and now every one are brilliant active Smolt, miniature Salmon in fact, and as different fish from the duller and more inactive Parr as one could conceive."

BELONE VULGARIS, Flemm. The Gar-fish or Gar-pike.
Is occasionally taken off Weston.

SCOMBERESOX SAURUS, Walb.
The Skipper has been taken in Somersetshire. Mr. Dunn sent me a good example, 11 inches long, in September this year, which he observes "sprang into a fisherman's boat at midnight. I have known nearly a dozen similar instances."

EXOCETUS EVOLANS, Linn.   The Flying Fish.

Somersetshire.

ENGRAULIS ENCRASICHOLUS, Linn.   The Anchovy.

Occasionally taken in the shrimp-nets.   Those at the mouth of the Parret are said to be very superior.

CLUPEA HARENGUS, Linn.   The Herring; Whitebait (in part).

I obtained several small examples of this fish from the stationary shrimp-nets; but "Whitebait" is not taken to such an extent as to be an article of consequence as food.   I will here refer to some investigations which I made during the last two seasons, respecting *what Whitebait is*.   In May 1878 I commenced collecting examples, excluding other fishes as Gobies and Sticklebacks, a very few of which accidentally or fraudulently are found mixed with the true forms, restricting my observations to what are the species known by this name in London, to the trade, and to epicures.   My collections were continued until the end of October, all the examples coming from the Thames.   Mr. Charles, the Belgravian fishmonger, kindly procured me examples from the Medway during January and March this year, and subsequently I have reverted to Billingsgate for my supply.   I examined 138 of these fish taken during May and June 1878, the longest of which was 2·5 inches: about 1 in 10 were Sprats, the remainder the young of the Herring.   In August, out of 46 examples, from 2 to 3·5 inches in length, 24 (from 2 to 2·7 inches long) were Sprats, and 21 (from 2·8 to 3·5 inches long) were young Herrings.   In October, out of 41, from 2·5 to 3·5 inches long, all were Herrings.   It thus appears that both Sprats and young Herrings find their way into the London market as Whitebait.   Out of 31 examples of winter Whitebait received from Mr. Charles, 26 varied from 2 to 4·5 inches in length, the larger ones having well developed roe, all were Sprats; the remaining 5 were young Herrings from 5 to 7·5 inches long, the largest possessing slightly developed roe.

That Pennant's drawing was the Whitebait of the present time there can be but little doubt, as well as that his examples were young Herrings.   It is also certain that Donovan's figure is that of a young Shad, the immature of which, if sufficiently numerous, would do as well as those of the Herring or of the Sprat; while I certainly possess the young of these last two forms which I have received as Whitebait.

CLUPEA ALOSA, Cuv.   The Shad or Allis Shad.

CLUPEA FINTA, Cuv.   The Twaite Shad.

A good local example exists in the Weston Museum.   At the commencement of June these fish were common in the Severn near Gloucester, while their ova was ripe.   They used to ascend far above Shrewsbury, and many were captured on the fords in the river Severn; but for years none have been seen, probably owing to the weirs on that river and their being unable to ascend the fish-passes; while for the last few seasons I understand that they have greatly decreased in numbers in the Wye.   As the floods at the earlier part of this year entirely precluded their capture at the mouth of the latter river, it is to be presumed that there will be an augmented supply in May and June 1880, should the season be favourable for fishing.

CLUPEA PILCHARDUS, Walb.   The Pilchard.   (Plate LXII. fig. 1.)

A few stragglers are said occasionally to be taken off Weston. Observing a great diversity in the various descriptions of this fish, I applied to Mr. Dunn of Megavissey, who kindly forwarded me about a dozen, one half of which were spotted along the sides, the remainder being spotless.   The following are the various formularies given for this fish :—

Donovan.   D. 18, P. 16, V. 8, A. 17, C. 32.   (L. l. shown as distinct in figure, with about 31 scales.)
Yarrell.   B. viii.   D. 18, P. 16, V. 8, A. 18, C. 19.   Scales "very large."
Cuv. & Val. D. 17, P. 17, V. 6, A. 21, C. 18, L. l. 29.   Cæc. pyl. innumerable.
Conch.   D. 18, P. 16, V. 8, C. 22, L. l. (about 37 in figure).
Günther.   B. vi.   D. 17–18, V. 6, A. 18–19, L. l. 47–48. Cæc. pyl. 7.

Thus the number of scales along the body in this fish vary according to different authors from 29 to 48; the ventral fin rays from 6 to 8, and the cæcal appendages between "seven" and "innumerable."   Taking some fine examples of Pilchards sent to me by Mr. Matthias Dunn, I found them as follows :—

D. 18, P. 19, V. 8, A. 17–18, C. 19, L. l. 29–30, L. tr. 9.

Cæc. pyl. numerous.   From 17 to 19 scutes before the base of the ventral fin, and 14 posterior to it.   The proportions being shown in the figure (Plate LXII.), it is unnecessary to advert to them.   The cæcal appendages were very numerous, and much shorter in some examples than in others.   The sole British *Clupea* that I have met with having only 7 appendages is *C. sprattus*, which, however, has 47–48 scales along the lateral line.   Therefore I cannot think that *Clupea sagax*, Jenyns, from the Pacific coast of America, Japan, and New Zealand, is "so closely allied to the European Pilchard that it might be more properly described as a climatal variety" (Günther, Catal. vii. p. 444); for though the number of dorsal and anal fin-rays is the same, instead of having L. l. 29–30, L. tr. 9, it has L. l. 50–54, L. tr. 13—a conclusive proof that the two ought not to be classed as varieties of one species.   However, I think I am now in a position to explain this remarkable discrepancy in the number of scales as given by various authors.   I received a scaleless (but otherwise beautiful) example of Pilchard, 8·3 inches in length, from Mr. Dunn,